the haven companion

the haven companion

Philip & Erin Ulrich

Published by Here We Go Productions, LLC, www.herewegoproductions.com.

ISBN-10: 0-9893852-5-6
ISBN-13: 978-0-9893852-5-1

Design and layout by Phil & Erin Ulrich, Design by Insight, www.designbyinsight.net.

Character illustrations by Annie Barnett, Be Small Studios, www.besmallstudios.com.

Contents

A Note from the Authors

We created *The Haven Companion* to help readers dig deeper into the story of *Haven*. Our hope is that it will create an even richer reading experience for you.

A downloadable answer key is available at:

www.thegrowlybooks.com/haven-key

Have fun!

Phil & Erin

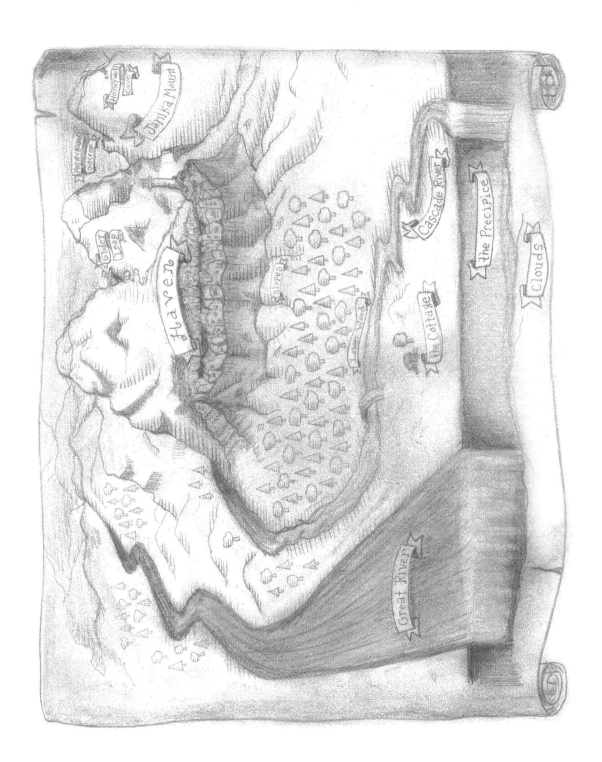

Ember

1
The Great River

> "Another clap of thunder echoed along the cliffs and seemed to shake the whole mountain. 'Hurry up, Growly!' Ember breathed. A twinge of worry was there under all the excitement. He would be all right though. Growly was a sensible bear, most of the time."
>
> - *Haven*, page 2

Let's Talk about the Story

1. What is the name of the place where the Great River comes out of the mountains?

2. What funny things does Ember remember about Growly?

3. What is Ember looking for up on Glider Leap?

4. Describe the weather while Ember is up on Glider Leap.

5. Why do you think Ember is so interested in finding the little blue and red bird?

Vocabulary

Look these words up in a dictionary and write the definitions.

venture _____

enormous _____

twinge _____

sensible _____

churn _____

haze _____

Draw a picture of Ember as the storm comes closer.

Names to Remember

The Great River - the wide river to the west of Haven

Hegel - the founder of Haven

Janika - Hegel's long lost love

The Lower Lands - the flat land below Haven

Glider Leap - the building up on Mount Hegel where gliders take off and land

Backland Valley - the valley behind Mount Hegel

Cascade River - the river that runs through the Backland Valley and down to The Precipice

The Banks - the land between the Cascade River and the Great River

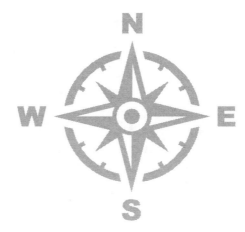

2
On Glider Leap

"Ember pushed on, gasping for breath as she made her way downward. Raindrops were all around now. Little splatters in the dust at first, joining with other splatters until the path was slick and wet. Ember's dress was soon soaked and clung about her as she ran, slipping and sliding on the muddy stones."

- Haven, page 10

Let's Talk about the Story

1. What does Ember get from the storage room in Glider Leap?

2. What does Ember think she saw across the Great River?

3. Describe how Ember is dressed.

4. Why is Ember hurrying down the mountain?

5. What happens to Ember as she gets close to the Lookout?

Vocabulary

Look these words up in a dictionary and write the definitions.

swivel _____

splatter _____

jolt _____

clamber _____

torrent _____

parapet _____

Names to Remember

The Lookout - the tower at the end of Haven
The Little Cliffs - the cliffs on which Haven is built

3
The Lookout

"On a clear day you could see for miles in all directions. Ash had once spotted an eagle above the trees on the other side of the Great River. And the Mayor had once seen a glider as far away as the Apple Valley, which was many, many miles to the east. In this storm though, there was nothing to see but twisting sheets of rain and bright flashes of lightning cutting through the gloom."

- Haven, page 18

Let's Talk about the Story

1. Who does Ember find at the Lookout?

2. Describe the main meeting room of the Lookout.

3. Why does Fergal want to go to the top of the Lookout?

4. Describe what the bears are able to see as they look out through the telescopes.

5. Why is Fergal so excited about opening the doors at the top of the Lookout.

Vocabulary

Look these words up in a dictionary and write the definitions.

lookout _____

queasy _____

spiral _____

gloom _____

blaze _____

The bears of Haven love to decorate everything with patterns and colors.
Decorate this telescope in your own style!

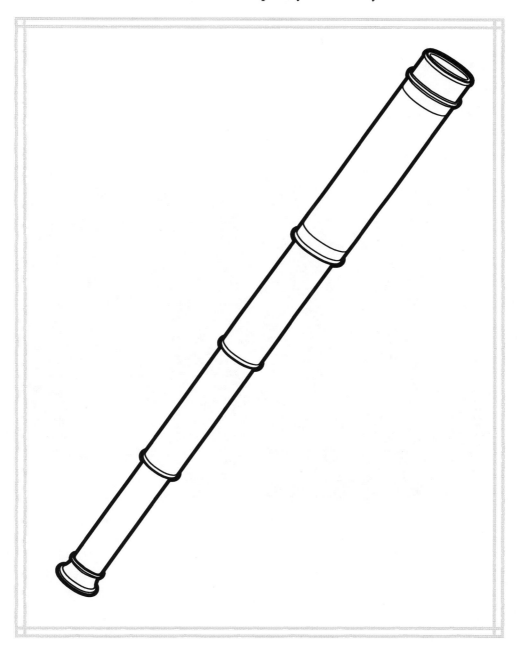

Names to Remember

Merridy - Ember's mother and the Haven librarian
Fergal - Growly's grandfather
Mika - Growly's grandmother

The Storm

> "'Pull it around!' he shouted to Adwin. The baker nodded and pulled the shutter until it finally began to swing. 'It's going to come around fast!' Farren cried as the wind suddenly caught the shutter and twisted it toward the window. The warning was almost too late, and Adwin had to scramble backward as the heavy wood whooshed by and slammed against the building with a jarring thud."
>
> - *Haven*, page 26

Let's Talk about the Story

1. Describe Ember's friends, Skye and Gittel.

2. What has taken place at the library?

3. Describe what is happening as the group of bears comes into Haven.

4. What are Farren and Adwin preparing to do when Merridy and the group meet them in the library?

5. For what is Gittel's mother famous?

Vocabulary

Look these words up in a dictionary and write the definitions.

flail _____

perch _____

reassure _____

scramble _____

clamor _____

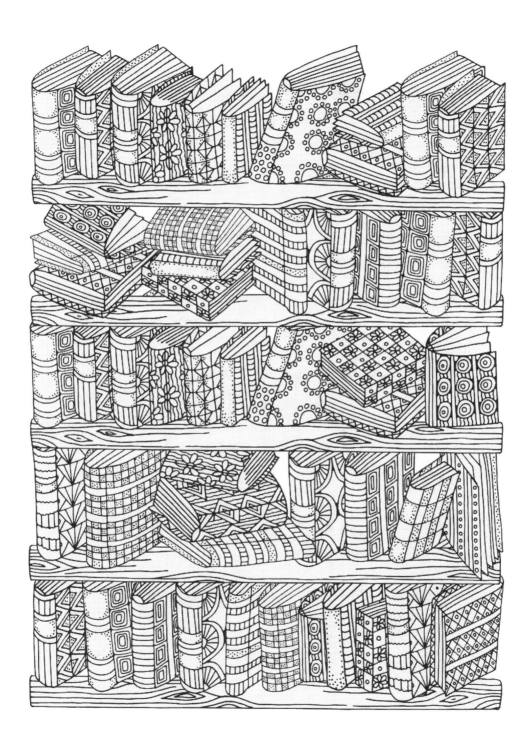

Names to Remember

Gittel - Ember's friend who loves to cook
Skye - Ember's friend who loves flying
Adwin - Gittel's father
Farren - Growly's father

5 Legends

> "This was her favorite place. Sitting right here on the couch with Merridy, sipping tea and talking in the quiet hours before bed. Usually the shutters were open, and on clear nights the sky was bright and bristling with stars. When the moon was full, the Lower Lands were bathed in a silvery glow, so bright that even at midnight you could see all the way to The Precipice."
>
> - Haven, page 29

Let's Talk about the Story

1. Where are Merridy and Ember at the start of this chapter?

2. Why is this Ember's favorite place?

3. Describe how Ember came to be with Merridy.

4. What do Merridy and Ember call the book, *Hegel the Mighty*?

5. What do do you think Merridy's quote, "*Time turns a turnip into honeycake,* and everyday heroes into legends," means?

Vocabulary

Look these words up in a dictionary and write the definitions.

wisp _____

legend _____

turnip _____

farfetched _____

Draw an illustration you might find in the book, *Hegel the Mighty*.

Write your own funny legend about Hegel.

6

Into the Night

> "The wind howled up from the Lower Lands, driving pelting, stinging rain up the side of Mount Hegel. It was slow going and dangerous. The pathway was fairly wide, but the force of the storm made the little groups stumble and sway as they journeyed downward. The Little Cliffs were only little when you compared them to The Precipice ..."
>
> - *Haven*, page 38

Let's Talk about the Story

1. Who is at the front door, and what instructions does he give Ember and Merridy?

2. Explain what the Rescue Committee is.

3. Who are the missing bears?

4. How many bears of the Rescue Committee volunteer to go and search?

5. Write as many words as you can find in this chapter that describe *storm*, *wind,* and *rain*.

Vocabulary

Look these words up in a dictionary and write the definitions.

committee _____

podium _____

assume _____

cavern _____

boulder _____

Draw Ember, Merridy, and Skye as they travel to the Westwind Caverns.

Names to Remember

Merritt - a small cub who is missing with her grandfather
Wynton - Merritt's grandfather
Westwind Caverns - the caves at the base of the Little Cliffs

The Search

> "As they came to the top of the hill they were met with the roaring thunder of the Cascade River. The sound of it rose even above the noise of the storm. A flash of lightning lit the area all around them, and Ember gasped. 'Look at the size of it!' she cried. 'I have never seen it this full!'"
>
> - *Haven*, page 46

Let's Talk about the Story

1. Describe the large meeting room in the caverns.

2. What time is it when they reach the apple grove?

3. Why do they need to stay close together in the apple grove?

4. Why is Ember surprised when she sees the Cascade River?

5. Describe what happens to Skye as they come close to the river.

Vocabulary

Look these words up in a dictionary and write the definitions.

hearth _____

whimper _____

grove _____

hoarse _____

landmark _____

Draw a map of your house or backyard below. Have someone hide a toy or other item, and then you can set out on a search to find it!

8

Gittel's Pancakes

"The door swung wide, and Ember was pulled inside as Gittel wrapped her in a tight hug and then began to help her with her coat and pack. 'You're soaking!' Gittel said, and the next moment was calling, 'Mama! Blankets! We need blankets! And tea and …'"

- Haven, page 52

Let's Talk about the Story

1. How is Skye described at the beginning of this chapter, when she is sitting next to Ember in the cave?

2. What instructions does Farren give to Skye and Ember?

3. Where does Gittel live?

4. What are the two reasons Ember is excited when Gittel suggests having breakfast before they go to bed?

5. What color is Gittel's fur?

Vocabulary

Look these words up in a dictionary and write the definitions.

flicker _____

abandon _____

towering _____

exhaustion _____

With a parent's help, find a recipe for delicious pancakes and write it down.

Names to Remember

Fiana - Gittel's mother

Into the Air

"There was the sound of the thump of Ember's boots on the stone and the sound of the thump of her heartbeat in her ears, and then the wind caught the wings of the glider and she leapt out into the sky."

- Haven, page 61

Let's Talk about the Story

1. What does Ember notice when she wakes up?

2. Where do Ember, Skye, and Gittel go once they leave Gittel's home?

3. Describe Glider Leap.

4. What do the glider pilots say as they are taking off?

5. Why do you think it isn't safe to fly with binoculars all the time?

Vocabulary

Look these words up in a dictionary and write the definitions.

muffle _____

assistant _____

faulty _____

ancient _____

harness _____

Find the words hidden below. Hint: some are diagonal.

```
W  M  E  X  S  J  V  I  L  L  A  G  E  C  R  K  C
S  O  M  C  E  I  M  G  J  M  M  E  R  R  I  D  Y
K  A  E  E  M  E  R  E  A  C  T  E  L  M  R  Z  C
F  C  A  V  E  R  N  T  N  T  P  S  E  R  C  T  H
S  L  D  K  Y  X  H  D  I  R  T  U  A  L  B  B  C
J  L  O  Z  F  S  N  M  K  Q  H  Q  D  I  I  M  O
T  A  W  S  S  E  M  Z  A  J  D  M  E  B  A  P  P
M  U  A  B  G  O  A  D  V  E  N  T  U  R  E  B  A
B  S  R  E  C  C  P  H  A  V  E  N  S  A  R  Q  R
C  I  L  N  M  F  A  R  R  E  N  U  V  R  M  V  A
A  L  O  E  I  G  J  E  G  P  O  D  E  I  C  F  P
S  V  O  B  M  P  R  L  P  M  O  D  S  A  A  I  E
C  J  T  O  Y  B  E  H  R  Y  I  A  K  N  D  A  T
A  K  B  N  K  G  E  O  K  L  M  L  Y  V  W  N  V
D  P  O  K  E  O  N  R  G  K  H  I  E  H  I  A  C
E  M  X  H  O  E  U  B  H  T  O  R  R  E  N  T  S
B  Z  D  R  I  D  E  T  A  E  G  I  T  T  E  L  E
```

Hegel	torrent	Skye	Adwin
Janika	parapet	Gittel	Farren
glider	Haven	legend	village
Cascade	Lookout	committee	adventure
enormous	Merridy	cavern	Fiana
Ember	librarian		

Rescue

"Ember flew in twisting circles, following the torrent as it headed south and scanning the riverbanks for any sign of the lost bears. She had been searching for over an hour, gazing down through the binoculars for a while and then circling upward on the wind. The shadow of her glider raced along below her, speeding over the countryside in the bright morning sunlight."

- Haven, page 65

Let's Talk about the Story

1. Describe what the Cascade River looks like as Ember flies above it.

2. What is it that Ember sees flying past her?

3. Explain what Ember knows about eagles and about Goldentail.

4. How does Ember find Merritt?

5. Describe Ember's plan to get Wynton and Merritt back across the river.

Vocabulary

Look these words up in a dictionary and write the definitions.

fumble _____

unpredictable _____

flint _____

topple _____

sprawl _____

Would you like to fly in a glider? Tell about where you would go and the things you might see, or draw a picture.

Names to Remember

Goldentail - the eagle that comes to help Ember

The Day

> "The sun was coming up over the Lower Lands, filling the library with a warm, orange glow. One by one the bears turned out their lamps, and the sound of laughter and talking quieted for a moment as they all gazed out the tall library windows at the sunrise. It was a beautiful sight."
>
> - *Haven*, page 76

Let's Talk about the Story

1. Describe what happened in the two days after the rescue.

2. Why had Merridy visited the Honey Well?

3. Who does Ember meet in the hall of the library?

4. What do the bears eat for breakfast?

5. What funny thing does Fergal tell about Growly's father, Farren?

Vocabulary

Look these words up in a dictionary and write the definitions.

jagged _____

erupt _____

vague _____

splutter _____

Follow the directions below to make a bear face out of paper!
You'll need to start with a square piece to make it work.

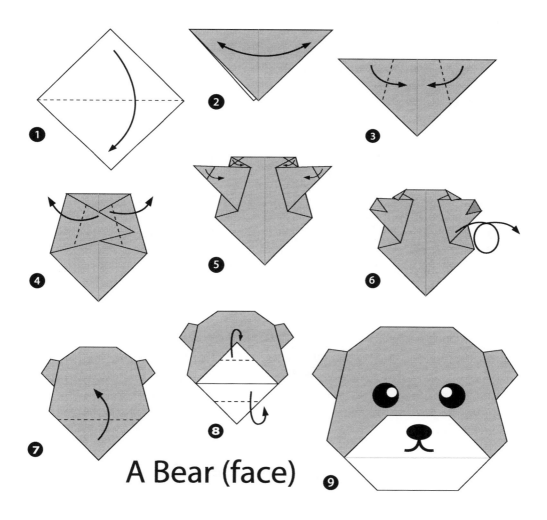

A Bear (face)

Names to Remember

Dugan - Skye's little brother

12

Adventure Ember, Adventure

"Ember looked over at Gittel and Skye as they joyfully sang along with the crowd, stretching out the final line of the chorus until everyone howled with laughter. Ember had sung the song hundreds of times, and she always loved it. Today though, she could feel an excitement bubbling up inside her that made every silly line of the song seem special and important."

- Haven, page 80

Let's Talk about the Story

1. What song does the Mayor suggest singing?

2. What do the rest of the bears reply, and what do they sing instead?

3. What advice does the Mayor have for Skye?

4. What extra items did Gittel bring with her in her pack?

5. What special items did Skye pack plenty of?

Vocabulary

Look these words up in a dictionary and write the definitions.

conversation _____

hysterical _____

bewilder _____

foothill _____

nudge _____

Draw a picture of Ember, Skye, Gittel, and the mayor next to the Lookout. Remember, the Lookout is a tall tower (a little bit like a lighthouse).

13
The Lower Woods

"As the forest closed in around her, Ember entered a world of shadows and bright beams of sunlight, piercing down though the leafy branches of the trees. Towering oaks and maples creaked in the brisk mountain breeze, and the sound of rustling leaves and birdcalls filled the air."

- *Haven*, page 85

Let's Talk about the Story

1. Describe the game that Cubs play in the Whispering Way.

2. Describe the way Ember set up her camp site.

3. What did Ember eat for her first meal on her Adventure?

4. Why do you think Merridy joked that Growly might empty Haven of notebooks?

5. What sounds does Ember hear in the forest?

Vocabulary

Look these words up in a dictionary and write the definitions.

evergreen _____

undergrowth _____

bough _____

chatter _____

In this chapter, Ember has to find her way through the Lower Woods to the place where she will make her camp. See if you can find your way through the maze below!

Names to Remember

The Whispering Way - a patch of tall ferns in the Lower Woods where Cubs like to play

The Lower Woods - the large forest in the Lower Lands where Ember camps during her Adventure

14

Things to do When You're Camping

"Ember let out a happy sigh as she caught sight of a little nest, high up in the branches of a nearby tree. There were two small babies in the nest, chirping excitedly as their mother nestled in between them. Ember had watched them hatch a few weeks ago, and she had been back every day since, noting how their feathers were coming in and guessing at their size."

- Haven, page 91

Let's Talk about the Story

1. What does Ember write about in her nature journal?

2. Describe Ember's new friends who come to visit.

3. Which bear had been the best in Haven at learning languages?

4. Merridy said, "Flowers need to get rained on if they want to grow tall." What do you think that means?

5. List some of the fun activities Ember does while camping.

Vocabulary

Look these words up in a dictionary and write the definitions.

dense _____

mysterious _____

conclusion _____

examine _____

bristle (verb) _____

Ember thought that the clouds looked like a squirrel riding in a wheelbarrow. Draw what you think that looked like.

Names to Remember

Squiggle - the baby rabbit Ember meets at her campsite

15
The Cub's Adventure Manual

> "She crossed over the dusty path that led through the Lower Lands. Gittel and Skye were somewhere out there, miles off to the east in the patches of forest that ran along the foot of the mountains. They would be out hiking tonight, too, trying not to fall in holes, and at some point, lying down and eating a piece of chocolate while tapping their boots together."
>
> *- Haven*, page 99

Let's Talk about the Story

1. What is the Great Night Hike?

2. What do boy Cubs do instead of the hike on their Adventures?

3. What food is Ember allowed to take on the hike?

4. Describe the funny tradition for eating chocolate.

5. Where does Ember plan to sleep after the first night of hiking?

Vocabulary

Look these words up in a dictionary and write the definitions.

stow _____

tradition _____

custom _____

manual _____

precious _____

What fun or silly traditions does your family have?

Follow the directions below to make an owl out of paper!
You'll need to start with a square piece to make it work.

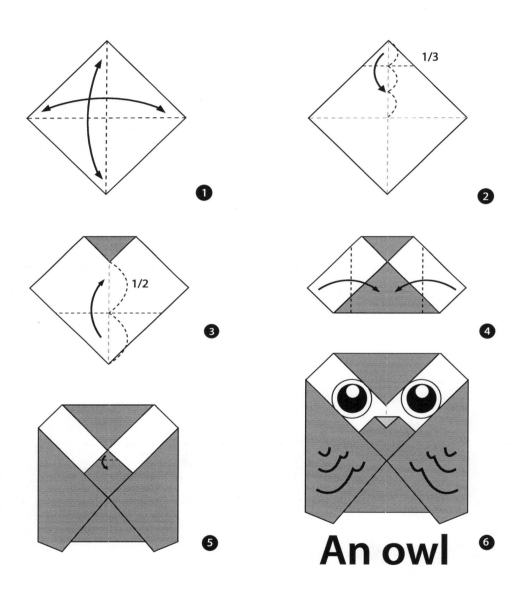

An owl

16
A Night by The Precipice

"Leaving the path, Ember crept quietly through the soft grass of the meadow, staying low as she came over the rise. A short way ahead of her, just past a big oak tree with a rope swing, stood a little cottage, quiet and peaceful in the early morning."

- *Haven*, page 106

Let's Talk about the Story

1. What do some bears say about The Precipice?

2. Explain what happened to C.J.

3. What three-word message did the little blue and red bird bring to
    Merridy many years before?

4. What did Farren say makes the Nights of Challenge such a challenge for
    boy Cubs?

5. Who does Ember see at the Cottage during her night hike?

Vocabulary

Look these words up in a dictionary and write the definitions.

horizon _____

propose _____

sandbag _____

recognize _____

extend _____

On her Adventure, Ember keeps a nature journal. Go outside (or look out your window) and write about or draw pictures of the different things you see.

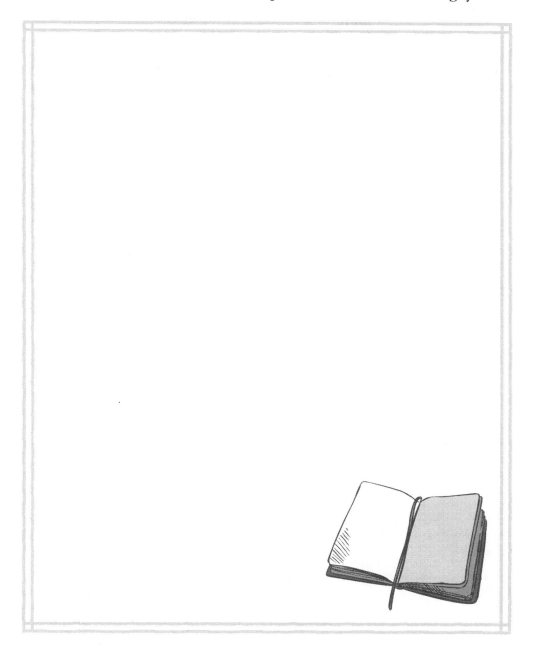

Names to Remember

Crispin Jacoby - C.J.'s full name

17
Goodbye to the Meadow

"'There is something about being out in the wild,' Merridy would say. 'Something that can catch up your heart and set it soaring. That's what you will find on your Adventure, Ember. Dreams and ideas that have been buried in the bustle will pop up all around you in the quiet, open spaces.'"

- Haven, page 111

Let's Talk about the Story

1. What is special about the place where Ember eats her sandwich on the third night of the hike?

2. Describe what will happen on the Day of Return.

3. How long has it been since the last Riverbed Day?

4. What will the bears search for on Riverbed Day?

5. What funny thing did Gittel try to cook on her Adventure?

Vocabulary

Look these words up in a dictionary and write the definitions.

grimy _____

dusk _____

rugged _____

cascade _____

nugget _____

Names to Remember

Heflin's Reach - a thin rocky island far out in the Great River
Calico and Laila - two of Ember's other girl Cub friends

18
The Day of Return

> "The street was filled with sounds of laughter and shouting, and Ember breathed deeply, taking in the delicious smell of fresh pies and hot bread. She could already see the long tables at the foot of the Lookout, piled high with mountains of food."
>
> - *Haven*, page 121

Let's Talk about the Story

1. What song do the bears sing as Ember and her friends return, and why do they sing it?

2. Describe what the little Cubs do during all the excitement.

3. What does Merridy tell Ember about C.J. and Fergal when they were younger?

4. How many gliders are the bears expecting to return?

5. Why are Merridy and Ember suddenly worried?

Vocabulary

Look these words up in a dictionary and write the definitions.

official _____

engulf _____

blissful _____

ruins _____

procession _____

Draw what you think a Terfuffenny Cake might look like. Make up a recipe.

19
Missing

> "Pushing hard to the right, Ember came swooping around
> the far side of the mountain, soaring out over Belden Valley
> with its carpet of wildflowers and sparkling lake. The last
> rays of sunlight were glistening on the smooth water,
> sending flickers of light across the valley as dusk settled in."
>
> - Haven, page 130

Let's Talk about the Story

1. Describe what happened the first time Ember and Growly met.

2. What is the bears' search plan?

3. Why are Merridy and Ember going to the Honey Well?

4. Who is going to search the valley Growly was assigned to for his Adventure?

5. Why do you think flying at night would be dangerous?

Vocabulary

Look these words up in a dictionary and write the definitions.

blurry _____

topple _____

launch _____

formation _____

current (air) _____

Gliders are an important part of life in Haven.
Make a paper airplane glider using the instructions below.

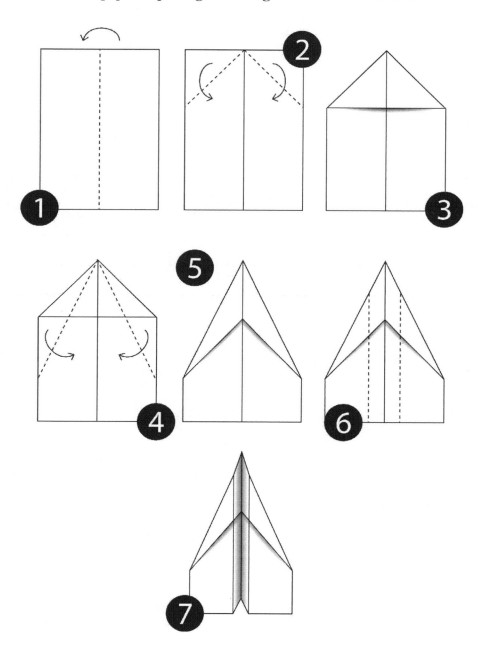

Names to Remember

Belden Valley - the valley on the side of Janika Mountain where the Honey Well cave is located

20
The Home of the Bees

> "Bears had been coming to the Honey Well since those ancient times, flying in from Glider Leap to collect honey. The bears of Haven were free to take as much as they needed. That's the way it had always been, since Hegel and his friends helped the bees by seeding the valley."
>
> - *Haven*, page 135

Let's Talk about the Story

1. Why are Ember and Merridy concerned that it is almost night?

2. Explain how the Honey Well cave came to be.

3. How do the bears and bees help each other?

4. How do the bees communicate?

5. What do the bees tell Merridy?

Vocabulary

Look these words up in a dictionary and write the definitions.

secure _____

wobble _____

lurk _____

crimson _____

chronicle _____

Follow the directions below to make a bee out of paper!
You'll need to start with a square piece to make it work.

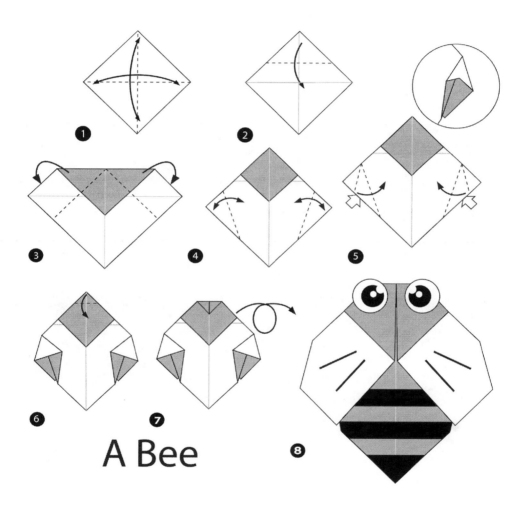

A Bee

21
Farren's Report

"Haven and Mount Hegel were still bathed in night. The piercing beams of morning light had not reached there yet, though the main street was filled with bears and the windows were lit. Ember could see tiny dots of lamplight moving out toward the Lookout and others heading down toward the pathway to the Lower Lands."

- *Haven*, page 144

Let's Talk about the Story

1. Describe the patterns on Skye's glider wing.

2. Ember tells Merridy she could never give up on Growly. When Ember says, "Now I really understand," what do you think she means?

3. Why do you think the light of sunrise hasn't reached Haven yet?

4. Who will be the only ones at Riverbed Day this year?

5. Why does Farren tell Ember and Skye not to fly too close to the Great River?

Vocabulary

Look these words up in a dictionary and write the definitions.

familiar _____

determination _____

ripple _____

region _____

loom (verb) _____

Decorate Skye's glider wing like it is described in this chapter.

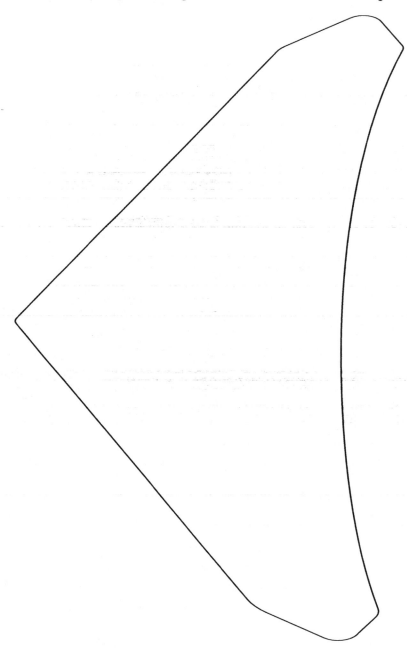

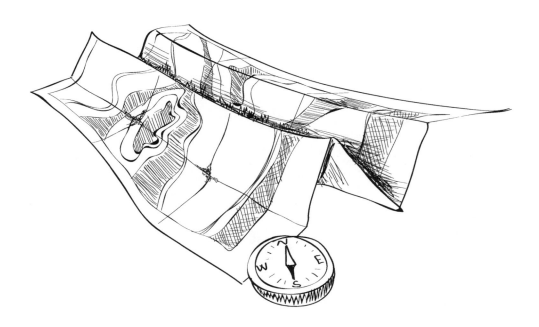

22
Goldentail

> "There were bears up on the gates, peering down into the dry riverbed and checking the bracings and joints. It was the Building Committee. They were in charge of the maintenance of the gates and of all the designs and devices that helped the village in the heights. They had been up here all week, working and testing and fixing anything that needed to be replaced."
>
> - *Haven*, page 150

Let's Talk about the Story

1. Ember is surprised by the sight of something she has never seen before. What is it?

2. Who is in charge of the River Gate?

3. What chilly summer tradition is Ember reminded of?

4. What do you think Skye might have seen across the Great River?

5. What does Goldentail do that astonishes Ember and Skye?

Vocabulary

Look these words up in a dictionary and write the definitions.

brace (verb) _____

cistern _____

gemstone _____

cog _____

spotter _____

Find the words hidden below. Hint: some are diagonal.

```
C B H L H Z F S F B A C K P A C K
O O V F Y P G E L S D D G M B C C
R O Y Z T N L P R F S S S T U P U
P T W L L G I A P U O X T D K G B
A S U Q G R L O D M W S H O E G H
F A W I E U G G U U W Y N T O N H
X H U Z C R I S P I N N X N R K O
K Q A O M C A Q G L O D T G E B R
S I N T V L B V H I O M M O S V I
M I X N J B O K T W G V E L C P Z
B O I I M U I I M B Y O R D U A O
V A F G P A D E V E R G R E E N N
N F E R N A Y P S A O P I N S C T
W S X S R Y M O Q R Y W T T D A S
L A N T E R N I R S T X T A C K I
F L O O D F V A L L E Y I I S E M
I M T Y X M A N U A L N A L J S Z
```

Goldentail lantern   rescue   horizon
Wynton   pancakes   fern   Crispin
Merritt   binoculars evergreen mayor
boots   backpack   tradition bears
valley   Cub   manual   flood
Squiggle

Names to Remember

Ruslan - the leader of the Building Committee
Pepper - Ruslan's daughter

Draw Ember and Skye flying their gliders over the mountains.

23
The Danger in the Peaks

"With Goldentail in the lead, they sped into the canyon, turning hard around a long bend with the river roaring underneath. As they came around the bend, Ember let out a cry. An avalanche!"

- Haven, page 157

Let's Talk about the Story

1. Why does Ember fly up high at Flarian's Pass?

2. Why has Ember flown in this area many times before?

3. Describe the canyon into which Goldentail leads them.

4. Why is the avalanche so dangerous for the bears of Haven?

5. What happens to Skye and Ember's gliders?

Vocabulary

Look these words up in a dictionary and write the definitions.

boulder _____

landmark _____

canyon _____

avalanche _____

wrench (verb) _____

The canyon near Flarian's Pass is a beautiful place where the Cubs of Haven go camping in the summer for the Night Amongst the Peaks. Color this picture and draw a Cub taking a swim in the icy river.

Names to Remember

Flarian's Pass - a lower place in the mountain peaks that can be seen from Glider Leap

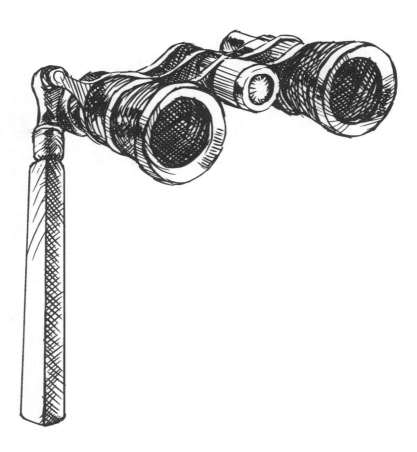

24
The Help of Friends

"Gittel usually did her best to stay away from gliders, and her landings were a big part of the reason. One side of the glider poked up from the rocks at a funny angle, and even from this distance, Ember could see torn fabric flapping in the breeze."

- *Haven*, page 164

Let's Talk about the Story

1. How is Skye in trouble?

2. Where do Skye and Ember stop to rest?

3. Why does Gittel do her best to stay away from gliders?

4. Gittel doesn't like flying, but what does she do really well that helps Skye and Ember?

5. Which way do the girls decide to go for help?

Vocabulary

Look these words up in a dictionary and write the definitions.

wreckage _____

outcrop _____

stammer _____

angle _____

current _____

Draw a picture of Gittel's rough landing or her swim to help Ember and Skye.

25
The Northern Cistern

> "Every Cub in Haven had to learn the basics of how the river gates worked, and they all had to memorize the maps of the twisting tunnels and caverns. *A bear should know a little about a lot, before they learn a lot about a little.* It was a saying from way back before Hegel's time, and it was the way Cubs were taught from the time they were very small."
>
> - *Haven*, page 170

Let's Talk about the Story

1. What was the biggest building project in the history of Haven?

2. What saying from before Hegel's time explains the way Cubs are taught?

3. What funny thing does Skye say about Gittel's love of water?

4. What instructions does Ruslan give when he sees the danger coming from the avalanche?

5. Why can't Ruslan open the river gates right away?

Vocabulary

Look these words up in a dictionary and write the definitions.

waterwheel _____

pulley _____

pinion _____

clamber _____

inlet _____

Help Ember, Skye, and Gittel find their way through the tunnels.

26
Riverbed Day

"Ember and Gittel took off at a run, racing across the walkway that ran along the top of the gates. She could see the surging wave on the lake, a swirling froth of mud and ice tossing a jumble of logs and branches as it rose higher. Ember hurried up a short flight of stairs. Gittel was right behind her, gasping and panting as they ran with all their strength."

- Haven, page 178

Let's Talk about the Story

1. How long will it take Skye to warn the bears who are in the riverbed?

2. How many stairs are there leading up to the signal room?

3. What do Ember and Gittel do to warn the bears of Haven about the coming danger?

4. What two things does Skye do to warn the mothers and the little Cubs?

5. Describe what it is like on the river gates when Ember and Gittel return from the signal room.

Vocabulary

Look these words up in a dictionary and write the definitions.

froth _____

billow _____

chaos _____

surge _____

strewn _____

Follow the directions below to make a rabbit face out of paper!
You'll need to start with a square piece to make it work.

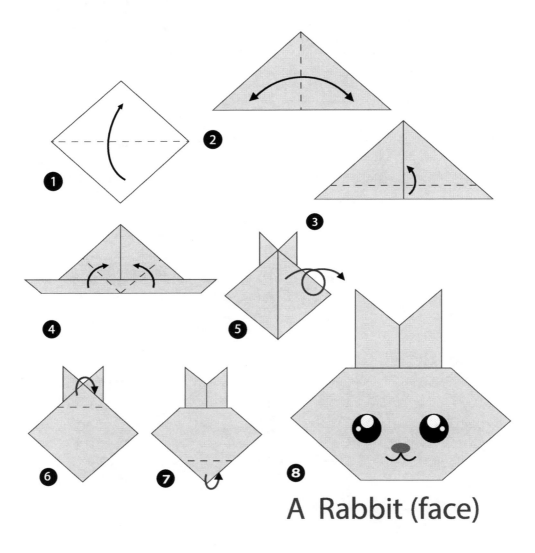

A Rabbit (face)

Gone

> "'He's gone!' Ember croaked, tears welling up as she pressed her face against Merridy's cheek. 'Mama ... he's gone!' Merridy squeezed Ember tighter, fighting back tears of her own as she tried to speak. Her mind was searching for the right thing to say, but nothing seemed to come."
>
> - *Haven*, page 190

Let's Talk about the Story

1. Describe the damage to the river gates.

2. How do Ember and Gittel plan to get back to Haven?

3. Who meets Ember and Gittel when they reach the Lookout?

4. What news does Growly's mother, Edolie, have for Ember?

5. Where do the bears plan to search the following day?

Vocabulary

Look these words up in a dictionary and write the definitions.

satisfaction _____

occasionally _____

trace _____

makeshift _____

strain _____

Find the words hidden below. Hint: some are diagonal.

```
C  X  X  V  V  W  R  E  C  K  A  G  E  M  B  V  T
Q  N  H  E  J  H  B  T  D  Q  T  W  U  D  E  P  X
S  E  K  C  D  A  N  G  E  R  P  V  T  J  O  D  L
U  U  C  L  I  E  W  S  A  Q  R  G  E  K  H  L  D
C  M  N  H  R  S  D  G  C  N  E  E  R  W  E  W  J
O  B  O  R  O  D  T  C  B  E  C  M  F  Q  O  E  B
T  S  O  U  I  C  W  E  P  F  I  S  U  F  I  O  A
T  T  F  H  N  S  O  W  R  R  P  T  F  S  O  C  C
A  X  E  R  S  T  E  L  A  N  I  O  F  H  J  J  K
G  P  X  L  B  B  A  O  A  W  C  N  E  P  E  U  L
E  I  B  Z  E  T  S  I  U  T  E  E  N  L  D  J  A
B  N  R  K  F  S  G  F  N  V  E  B  N  A  O  M  N
J  E  I  X  A  N  C  U  I  S  H  E  Y  T  L  V  D
U  C  D  M  I  K  A  O  U  R  J  L  U  F  I  N  R
E  O  G  R  O  W  L  Y  P  B  E  D  Q  O  E  Q  X
C  N  E  E  I  R  W  A  P  E  A  E  W  R  F  Y  X
C  E  R  I  V  E  R  B  E  D  Z  N  Z  M  N  Q  J
```

telescope	**sunrise**	Edolie	gemstone
cottage	**fire**	platform	Mika
chocolate	**riverbed**	Belden	soar
Precipice	**pinecone**	danger	torrent
mountains	**Terfuffenny**	Backland	wreckage
bridge	**Growly**	cistern	

28
A Message in the Night

"The library was quiet and still, bathed in warm, glowing moonlight coming through the windows. Ember tossed restlessly on her mattress, which was laid out next to Merridy's in the middle of the library floor. They often spent the night here, surrounded by the books and the light of the stars that glistened above the clouds stretching out beyond The Precipice."

- Haven, page 193

Let's Talk about the Story

1. Describe where Merridy and Ember decide to sleep.

2. What happens in Ember's dream?

3. How is Ember's dream interrupted?

4. What surprise does the little bird bring?

5. What is Merridy asked to do?

Vocabulary

Look these words up in a dictionary and write the definitions.

glisten _____

glimmer _____

dismay _____

scribble _____

silhouette _____

Write what is written on the note the bird brings to Merridy.

For Growly

> "There was a strong breeze up on the platform, fresh with the smell of ice as it blew in from the mountains. There was a hint of fall in that smell and a chill that sent a shiver down Ember's back."
>
> - *Haven*, page 204

Let's Talk about the Story

1. Who are the first bears that Merridy and Ember decide to tell the news?

2. What is Merridy wearing as she runs out into the street?

3. What tasks does Edolie give to Calico and Laila?

4. What did the doctor say about Skye's injury?

5. What clothes does Gittel give to Ember at Glider Leap?

Vocabulary

Look these words up in a dictionary and write the definitions.

wheeze _____

astonishment _____

earnest _____

flicker _____

The bears of Haven love their slippers. They decorate them with bright patterns and are continually working on new designs. Color Merridy's slippers and draw some designs of your own.

30
Night Flight

> "All of a sudden, one of Ember's trembling paws slipped from the bar, and the glider lurched sharply to the left, sending her speeding through the darkness toward the cliffs. She let out a panicked cry, looking around wildly to try and see anything in the darkness."
>
> - *Haven*, page 208

Let's Talk about the Story

1. Describe the dangers of a night flight.

2. What happens when Ember is about to crash into the cliffs?

3. Why is landing a glider at the River Gate tricky?

4. Why does Ruslan decide to close the damaged river gates again, even though it's risky?

5. What color is the flag used to signal that the gates should be closed?

Vocabulary

Look these words up in a dictionary and write the definitions.

lurch _____

gorge _____

crest _____

gasp _____

din _____

Landing a glider at the River Gate can be very tricky.
Help this glider make a safe landing.

Find the words hidden below. Hint: some are diagonal.

```
R  R  D  F  A  M  I  L  Y  K  D  N  S  D  D  G  H
X  C  H  E  E  R  H  M  M  O  H  W  P  L  T  T  S
M  B  X  I  W  O  F  L  L  S  O  K  C  K  R  J  Q
O  J  J  W  P  I  R  T  A  D  K  I  B  Y  E  H  X
D  A  M  A  G  E  E  Y  A  V  K  K  S  V  E  X  K
U  S  J  R  V  M  C  H  I  P  P  I  N  G  T  O  N
A  W  A  M  M  H  S  E  P  J  T  S  O  N  O  V  L
W  O  J  U  E  D  A  A  I  H  L  D  W  H  P  J  R
E  O  L  K  H  S  N  N  G  I  Z  J  F  I  S  A  S
D  P  N  T  V  A  S  I  D  S  B  C  L  S  Z  R  C
D  K  I  Q  L  U  L  A  Y  W  D  M  A  T  G  B  P
I  X  P  S  P  P  D  N  G  F  R  X  K  O  K  O  E
N  S  U  J  M  N  R  N  J  E  X  I  E  R  J  O  P
G  R  K  A  W  K  E  I  T  O  S  F  T  Y  L  K  P
U  V  L  R  L  B  S  L  S  U  P  P  L  I  E  S  E
V  W  F  C  N  H  S  Y  Z  H  Z  E  R  V  N  T  R
I  T  F  I  G  U  R  E  S  K  L  F  L  A  G  G  K
```

Ruslan	family	flag	cheer
Pepper	message	plummet	snowflake
Ash	handwriting	swoop	Chippington
books	supplies	treetops	Annily
history	dress	lamplight	wedding
shadows	damage	figures	

31
The Plummet

"Ember felt panic welling up inside of her. How long had the gates been closed? Fifteen minutes? Half an hour? In all the commotion she had lost track of the time. What if it wasn't enough for Growly and C.J. to make it? What if the little bird hadn't been able to return Merridy's message in time?"

- *Haven*, page 214

Let's Talk about the Story

1. When the bears closed the gates again, why did the river rise quickly?

2. What is Ruslan most concerned about?

3. List the different signal flags and what they mean.

4. What is Ember sent off in her glider to do?

5. What is the Plummet?

Vocabulary

Look these words up in a dictionary and write the definitions.

plummet _____

overflow _____

tremor _____

hoist _____

plunge _____

The bears of the Building Committee use flags to signal each other at the River Gate. Add colors and patterns to these flags and write what each one might mean.

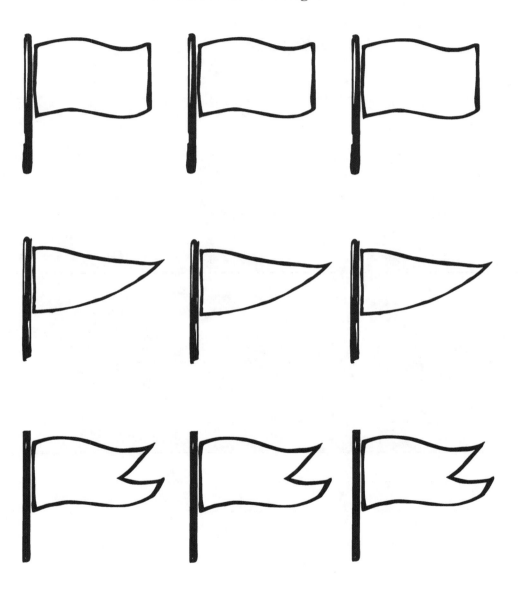

Return

> "Minutes passed, and they seemed like hours to Ember. She kept waiting to hear the roar of the river somewhere back behind her, but as the time stretched on, the only sound was the grunts and gasps of the bears as they ran, and the pounding of their boots as they came into the narrows."
>
> - Haven, page 223

Let's Talk about the Story

1. Why is Ember so concerned when she sees lantern light out in the riverbed?

2. Who is assigned to stay and watch at the bridge?

3. Describe how Merridy must have felt as she watched the figures trying to get out of the riverbed.

4. Describe how Growly looks when Ember sees him.

5. Write down what you think Merridy and C.J. might have said when they saw each other for the first time after so many years.

Vocabulary

Look these words up in a dictionary and write the definitions.

dismay _____

fumble _____

familiar _____

jumble _____

absentminded _____

Color the hidden meadow and add a beautiful sunrise.

33
What Lies across the River

> "A twirling flicker of white danced past Ember's nose, swirling up into the sky for a moment before twisting down across the platform of Glider Leap."
>
> - *Haven*, page 231

Let's Talk about the Story

1. Who are Chippy and Annily?

2. Why is Chippy so excited about the snowflake?

3. Why did the mayor have to ask the bears of Haven to give Chippy and Annily time to rest?

4. What are some of the things C.J. has been doing since he returned?

5. What does Ember realize about Growly?

Vocabulary

Look these words up in a dictionary and write the definitions.

abuzz _____

accent _____

recover _____

delight _____

propose _____

Follow the directions below to make a snowflake out of paper!
You'll need to start with a square piece to make it work.

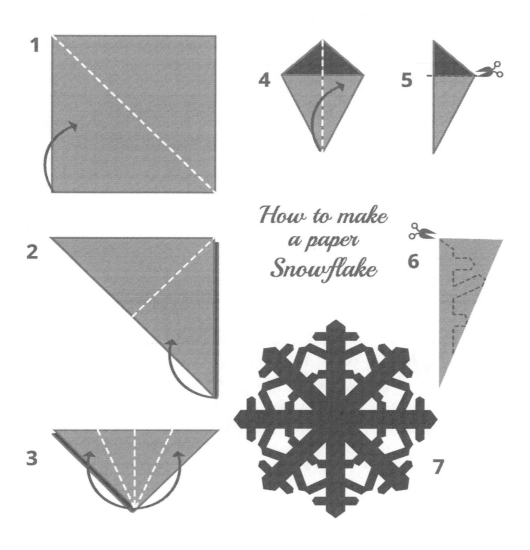

How to make a paper Snowflake

Names to Remember

Chippy - Growly's monkey friend who traveled with him up The Precipice (also known as Chippington)

Annily - a girl monkey from Chippy's village

34
Family

> "The smell of fall was in the air, and the trees were beginning to blaze with bright orange and red and yellow. And then would come the snow, and the long, frosty winter with open fires and hot tea and ... family. Ember felt her heart leap and the smile on her face spread wider. *My* family."
>
> - Haven, page 242

Let's Talk about the Story

1. Describe how Growly, Ember, and her friends are dressed for the wedding.

2. What is the traditional wedding song? What song do Merridy and C.J. want sung instead?

3. Something special happens after Merridy walks out of the cottage. What is it?

4. What is Gittel's mother worried about?

5. Describe Embers thoughts about Haven as she is walking home.

Vocabulary

Look these words up in a dictionary and write the definitions.

wistful _____

elegant _____

pantry _____

twilight _____

Draw a picture of the wedding with gliders dropping flower petals from above.

Join the Growly Club for FREE
and get exclusive access to:

behind the story videos

early book release offers

downloads, printables, & newsletters

and more Growly fun!

www.thegrowlyclub.com

Looking for the answers?

You can access the downloadable Answer Key here:

www.thegrowlybooks.com/haven-key

Made in the USA
Las Vegas, NV
28 June 2024

91611266R00083